KISS A ME

A Little Whale Watching

Babette Douglas

Illustrated by
Barry Rockwell

Kiss a me ™ ❤
Productions

Kiss A Me™ Productions, Inc. produces toys and booklets for children with an emphasis on love and learning. For more information on how to purchase a Kiss A Me collectible and plush toy or to receive information on additional Kiss A Me products, write or call:

Kiss a me™ Productions

Kiss A Me Productions, Inc.
90 Garfield Ave.
Sayville, NY 11782
888 - KISSAME
888-547-7263

About the Kiss A Me Teacher Creature Series:
This delightfully illustrated series of inspirational books by
Babette Douglas has won praise from parents and educators alike.
Through her wonderful "teacher creatures" she imparts profound lessons of tolerance
and responsible living with heartwarming insights and a humorous touch.

KISS A ME: A Little Whale Watching

Written by Babette Douglas
Illustrated by Barry Rockwell

ISBN 1-89034-308-0
Printed in China

www.kissame.com

To my favorite "Little Flower,"
Theresa M. Santmann

Preface

In our wonderful and ever-changing world,
children are our greatest legacy
and investment in the future.
And yet, in the world we have prepared for
them, love seems to have been mislaid.

With this little story, one of a series, one
little creature, Kiss A Me, seems to have
found love again and put it into action.

With an unshakable belief in kindness,
hope for a brighter future and a loving
desire to make a difference, Kiss A Me
teaches us all...that everyone can.

As your boat leaves the dock
And the land fades from view,
You head for deeper water
Where the whales wait for you.

Now, if whales could tell us,
Here's a story they might share
Of one very special whale
Who is waiting out there.

Far out on the ocean,
On a day just like this,
A little whale drifted,
Blowing seagulls a kiss.

He wiggled and laughed
And rolled all around
As he played in the ocean
In seaweed he'd found.

His mother dozed near him,
One ear to his play.
She sighed in contentment,
"What a clear, peaceful day."

Later she would ponder
For many a year:
When did the silent
Whale hunters appear?

His mother dove deep,
Deep, deep in the sea,
Calling out to her baby,
"Dive quickly to me!"

A net was thrown over
The little whale at play
To keep him from his mother
And from swimming away.

The hunters left quickly.
Mother had lured them away,
Away from her baby,
Netted while at play.

The little whale floundered,
Caught tight in the net.
He pushed and he pulled.
He struggled and wept.

"I will not be a captive
That performs every day.
I was born to be free.
I'm a mammal, not prey!"

"A fisherman, watching,
Called out as he drew near.
"You're okay, little whale.
They've not thrown a spear.

"Those men hunt these waters
With never a care.
They plunder and capture
Whatever is there.

"Yet, most people are loving.
Don't fear being alone.
I won't leave you netted.
I'm taking you home.

"I won't let them harm you.
Now don't pull away.
That net is too heavy.
You can't swim or play."

The little whale worried,
How bad might it get?
But the fisherman began
To cut free the net.

"You're just a little whale,
Too small to leave at sea,
So with this fishing line,
I'll tow you home with me."

In a safe harbor
The fisherman set him free.
The little whale rested
Before returning to the sea.

"Again I am free
To go where I wish.
To stay where I am
Or swim with the fish.

"First, I must find
The mother I miss,
To tell her I love her
And give her a kiss."

Far out to the ocean,
He swam all alone.
He called to his mother
To come bring him home.

Whales, when they call,
Send messages clear.
Sounds flash through the water
To other whales near.

Yet all that he met,
As he searched near and far,
Were broken toys, tires, trash,
Even oil and tar.

"What are they doing
To all I hold dear?
I'm still very little,
And I'm living in here."

Alone, he kept going,
Swimming fast with the tide.
He saw a great shadow
Draw close to his side.

He knew before seeing,
From the sounds he could hear,
The great whale approaching
Was his mother dear.

She too had been searching,
For lost from her side
Was this little whale,
Whom she loved with pride.

And once reunited,
They circled with glee,
Drew close together
And swam out to sea.

When she had fed him,
She nestled him near.
After resting together,
This truth she made clear.

"The water's polluted.
Don't stray from my side.
Some routes are still clear.
From the rest we must hide.

"Some men on earth hunt us.
Why? We don't know!
But swim now with caution
And stay deep below."

He listened with patience
And sweetly replied:
"I love you, dear mother,
But I must live free, not hide.

"Some people do love us!
To them I will go,
To ask their protection
For those living below.

"And we will reward them
For the good that they do,
By leaping and jumping
And loving them too.

"So on top of the water
I know I must stay.
I'll show all the people
I love them this way!"

For the rest of his life,
He'll swim in full view.
If you look, you may see him,
Blowing kisses at you.

Now whales are not named,
In the way of you and me.
They're named for the feelings
They bring to the sea.

This little whale's mother
Saw his love flowing free
And named him forever
My little whale, KISS A ME.

KISS A ME loves you...Pass it on!

THE END

Babette Douglas, a talented poet and artist, has written over 30 children's books in which diverse creatures live together in harmony, friendship and respect. She brings to her delightful stories the insights and caring accumulated in a lifetime of varied experiences.

"I believe strongly in the healing power of love," she says. "I want to empower children to see with their hearts and to love all the creatures of the earth, including themselves." The unique stories told by her "teacher creatures" enable children to learn to recognize their own gifts and to value tolerance, compassion, optimism and perseverance.

Ms. Douglas, who was born and educated in New York City, has lived in Sayville, New York for over forty years.

Additional Kiss A Me™ teacher-creature stories:

AMAZING GRACE

BLUE WISE

CURLY HARE

BLUFFALO Wins His Great Race

FALCON EDDIE

THE FLUTTERBY

KISS A ME Goes to School

KISS A ME To the Rescue

LARKSPUR

THE LYON BEAR™

THE LYON BEAR™ deTails

THE LYON BEAR™: The Mane Event

MISS EVONNE And the Mice of Nice

MISS TEAK And the Endorphins

NOREEN: The Real King of the Jungle

OSCARPUS

ROSEBUD

SQUIRT: The Magic Cuddle Fish

**Character toys are available for each book.
For additional information on books, toys,
and other products visit us at:**

www.kissame.com